TWO MONSTERS

09.

)15

To Carme Solé vendrell
and the mountain.

A Red Fox book

Published by Random House Children's Books
61-63 Uxbridge Road, London W5 5SA
a division of The Random House Group Ltd,
in Australia by Random House Australia (Pty) Ltd,
20 Alfred Street, Milson's Point, Sydney, NSW 2061, Australia,
in New Zealand by Random House New Zealand Ltd,
18 Poland Road, Glenfield, Auckland 10, New Zealand
and in South Africa by Random House (Pty) Ltd,
Endulini, 5A Jubilee Road, Parktown 2193, South Africa

First published by Andersen Press Limited 1985
Beaver Edition 1987
Red Fox edition 1991
5 7 9 10 8 6
© David McKee 1985
Printed and bound in Italy
THE RANDOM HOUSE GROUP Limited Reg. No.954009

www.**kids**at**randomhouse**.co.uk

ISBN 0 09 945530 7

TWO MONSTERS

David McKee

RED FOX

There was once a monster that lived quietly on the west side of a mountain.

On the east side of the mountain lived another monster.

Sometimes the monsters spoke together through a hole in the
mountain.

But they never saw each other.

One evening the first monster called through the hole, "Can you see how beautiful it is? Day is departing."

"Day departing?" called back the second monster. "You mean night arriving, you twit!"

"Don't call me a twit, you dumbo, or I'll get angry," fumed the first monster and he felt so annoyed that he could hardly sleep.

The other monster felt just as irritated and he slept very badly as well.

The next morning the first monster felt awful after such a bad night. He shouted through the hole, "Wake up, you numskull, night is leaving."

"Don't be stupid, you peabrain!" answered the second. "That is day arriving." And with that he picked up a stone and threw it over the mountain.

"Rotten shot, you fat ignoramus!" called the first monster as the stone missed him. He picked up a bigger stone and hurled it back.

That stone also missed. "Hopeless, you hairy, long-nosed nerk!" howled the second monster, and he threw back a rock which knocked the top off the mountain.

"You're just a stupid old wind-filled prune!" shouted the first monster as he heaved a boulder that knocked another piece off the mountain.

" Both of the monsters remained untouched but the mountain
was being knocked to pieces.

"You're a hairy, overstuffed, empty-headed, boss-eyed mess!" shouted the first monster as he threw yet another massive boulder.

"You're a pathetic, addlebrained, smelly, lily-livered custard tart!" screamed the second monster hurling a yet larger rock.

That rock finally smashed the last of the mountain and for the very first time the monsters saw each other.

This happened just at the beginning of another sunset.

"Incredible," said the first monster putting down the rock he was holding. "There's night arriving. You were right."

"Amazing," gasped the second monster dropping his boulder.
"You are right, it is day leaving."

They walked to the middle of the mess they had made to watch the arrival of the night and the departure of the day together.

"That was rather fun," giggled the first monster. "Yes, wasn't it," chuckled the second. "Pity about the mountain."

More Red Fox picture books
for you to enjoy

MUMMY LAID AN EGG
by Babette Cole 0099299119

THE RUNAWAY TRAIN
by Benedict Blathwayt 0099385716

DOGGER
by Shirley Hughes 009992790X

WHERE THE WILD THINGS ARE
by Maurice Sendak 0099408392

OLD BEAR
by Jane Hissey 0099265761

MISTER MAGNOLIA
by Quentin Blake 0099400421

ALFIE GETS IN FIRST
by Shirley Hughes 0099256053

OI! GET OFF OUR TRAIN
by John Burningham 009985340X

GORGEOUS!
by Caroline Castle and Sam Childs 0099400766

Other books by David McKee
in Red Fox

Prince Peter and the Teddy Bear
Charlotte's Piggy Bank
Isabel's Noisy Tummy
Not Now, Bernard
Mary's Secret
Tusk Tusk
Elmer
Elmer Again
Elmer on Stilts
Elmer and Wilbur
Elmer in the Snow
Elmer and the Wind
Elmer and the Lost Teddy
Elmer and the Stranger